A HAUNTED HOUSE STORYBOOK

THE HAUNTED TOOL SHED

BY RICK DETORIE

Watermill Press

For
Stephen

Dorrie and Zack were spending the last week of summer vacation on their grandfather's farm. They liked the farm because there were lots of fun places to play. They would play in the corn fields, in the barn, on the front porch, in the hen house, and in the tool shed.

"Don't go in the tool shed," said Grandpa shaking his head. "I don't want you playing in the tool shed."

"Okay, Grandpa," said Dorrie. "We'll go feed the chickens." She skipped toward the hen house, but Zack didn't go with her. He walked over to Grandpa and asked, "But why can't we play in the tool shed?"

"Because," said Grandpa.

"Because why?" said Zack.

"Because I don't want you to," said Grandpa.

"But why don't you want us to?" asked Zack.

Grandpa thought while he rubbed his chin. "Because there's a snurgle durgle hiding in the tool shed," said Grandpa. Then he turned and walked into the barn.

6

"A snurgle durgle?" said Zack to himself. "Wait until I tell Dorrie about this!"

Zack found Dorrie in the hen house, talking to the hens. "Do you know why Grandpa really doesn't want us to play in the tool shed?" he asked Dorrie.

"No, why?" asked Dorrie.

"Because," said Zack, "it's haunted! That's right. There's a big, ugly, terrible monster called a snurgle durgle living in there, and if we give him a chance, he'll grab us and gobble us up in his big, hairy old mouth!"

"Grandpa said that?!" exclaimed Dorrie.

"Just about," answered Zack.

"Well then, I'm staying out of the tool shed," said Dorrie.

All day long Zack thought about the snurgle durgle. The more he thought about it, the bigger and uglier it got. He wanted to sneak into the tool shed to take a look at it, but he was afraid that Grandpa would catch him.

How would you feel about a monster living in your house?

Finally, that night, after Dorrie and Zack went to bed on the back porch, Zack couldn't stand it anymore. He had to see the snurgle durgle. He asked Dorrie if she would go to the tool shed with him. *What would you do if you were Dorrie? Go or Stay?*

"Oh, you're so silly," said Dorrie. "There's no such thing as a snurgle durgle. Grandpa just told you that because he doesn't want you in his tool shed. Now go to sleep!"

But Zack didn't go to sleep. Instead, he took a flashlight and a broomstick, and sneaked off to the shed.

He carefully opened the creaky old door and stepped into the tool shed. It was cool and quiet inside. Flashing the light along the walls, Zack saw shovels, axes, wrenches, and rakes. On the floor were two dusty wooden boxes, too small to hide a full-grown snurgle durgle. Where could it be?

Where do you think?

Zack shined the light up to the ceiling. There were beams hanging below the ceiling. Long pieces of wood were laying on the beams. Maybe the snurgle durgle was up there. Zack gently poked the broomstick between the planks of wood.

Suddenly, a long, skinny arm swung from the ceiling. There it was, the snurgle durgle! Its big, hairy face was looking right into the light.

Zack screamed and raced out of the tool shed. He ran across the yard, leapt up the steps of the back porch, and dove into his sleeping bag.

"What happened?" cried Dorrie.

"The snurgle durgle!" gasped Zack. "I saw it! It tried to grab me and eat me!"

"Wow!" said Dorrie. "Let's get Grandpa. He'll get the snurgle durgle for you."

"No!" said Zack. "Don't tell Grandpa! I don't want him to know that I went into the shed after he told me not to. Promise you won't tell!"

would you tell?

Dorrie promised and she and Zack didn't mention the snurgle durgle or go near the tool shed for the rest of their visit on the farm. At the end of the week they went back to their home in the city.

School started, the weather turned cool, and soon it was
Zack's birthday.

On the day of his birthday party Zack received a large package in the mail. It was a birthday present.

What do you think the present is?

On top of the present was a note. It read:

Zack tore open the package and there it was – his birthday
present, THE SNURGLE DURGLE!